DEAR BA...

WE WISH ...

IN LIFE! YOU ARE LOVED BY <u>SO</u> MANY.

ALWAYS REMEMBER, THAT IS THE

ONLY THING THAT REALLY MATTERS. ☺

WITH MUCH LOVE,

JOHN & KARLA CANAVAN

MARCH 2015

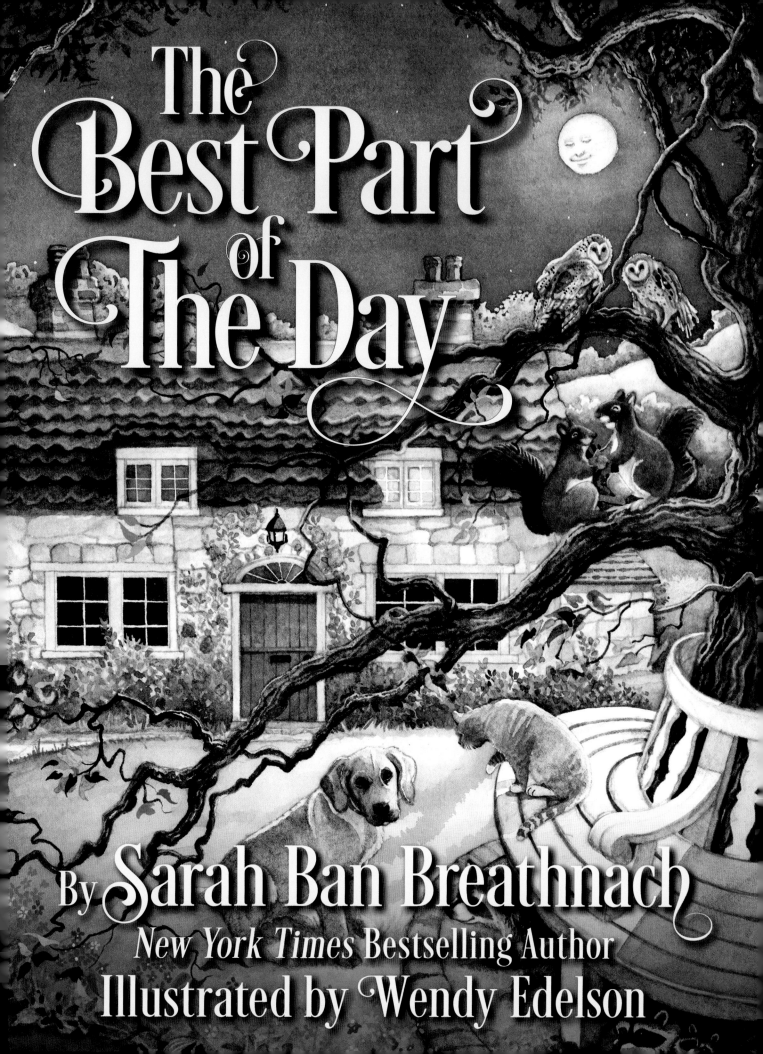

The Best Part of The Day

By Sarah Ban Breathnach

New York Times Bestselling Author

Illustrated by Wendy Edelson

Library of Congress Control Number: 2014944650
ISBN 978-1-62157-252-7

Published in the United States by Regnery Kids
An imprint of Regnery Publishing
A Salem Communications Company
300 New Jersey Avenue NW
Washington, DC 20001
www.RegneryKids.com

Manufactured in the United States of America
10 9 8 7 6 5 4 3 2 1

Books are available in quantity for promotional or premium use.
For information on discounts and terms, please visit our website: www.Regnery.com.

Distributed to the trade by
Perseus Distribution
250 West 57th Street
New York, NY 10107

For Kate,
the best part of every day.
With Love

I sigh that kiss you,
For I must own
That I shall miss you
When you have grown.
–WILLIAM BUTLER YEATS

Outside the window,
out past the lawn,
sweet night was snuggling
soft as a yawn.

All small ones home now
to burrow, to hedge, to nest.
All babes in bed now
for cuddles, stories, and rest.

Each part of the year
brings lots of good reasons
to treasure the gifts
we find in each season.

As we climb into bed
get ready to play
our favorite game called
"the best part of the day"!

Autumn paints all the leaves
yellow, orange, red, and brown.
Gusty winds make them dance
from the trees to the ground.

Squirrels gather their acorns
and build leafy warm nests.
Flocks of geese travel south
for a long winter's rest.

As this autumn day closes
we have stories to tell
as the bright harvest moon
holds us under its spell.

Snuggle up safe and warm,
as stars twinkle and play.
It's time to remember
the best part of the day.

Was it riding the bus
or recess-time races?

Was it getting our pumpkins
or painting their faces?

Was it picking the apples
or eating the pie?

Was it raking the leaves
or jumping so high?

So many fun days
while leaves are still falling.
There are more yet in store
when winter comes calling.

Jack Frost's winter visits
are always a treat,
when the snow is so deep
you can't see your feet.

Let's build a snowman
with buttons for eyes,
a cute carrot nose,
and a scarf for a tie.

When this winter day fades,
we have stories to share,
so crawl into bed
or pull up a chair.

Snuggle up safe and warm
as stars twinkle and play.
It's time to remember
the best part of the day.

Was it feeding the birds
while they chirp and tweet?
It's how birdies say
"thanks" for the treat!

Was it warming your hands
by the fire so bright?
Marshmallows and cocoa
on a cold, snowy night?

The choices are endless.
So full of good cheer,
let's turn the page now
for springtime is near.

Now spring has arrived
with sunshine and showers,
lots of fresh air,
and plenty of flowers.

There's a nest near the swing
and the whole world is new.
If you look for surprises
you'll find quite a few.

As night closes in,
our spring day now done,
new tales of adventure
have almost begun.

Snuggle up safe and warm
as stars twinkle and play.
It's time to remember
the best part of the day.

Was it tending the garden
with the sun shining bright?

Was it finding the chicks
when they hid out of sight?

Was it bringing in hay
and feeding the sheep?

Or cuddling sweet lambs
till they fell fast asleep?

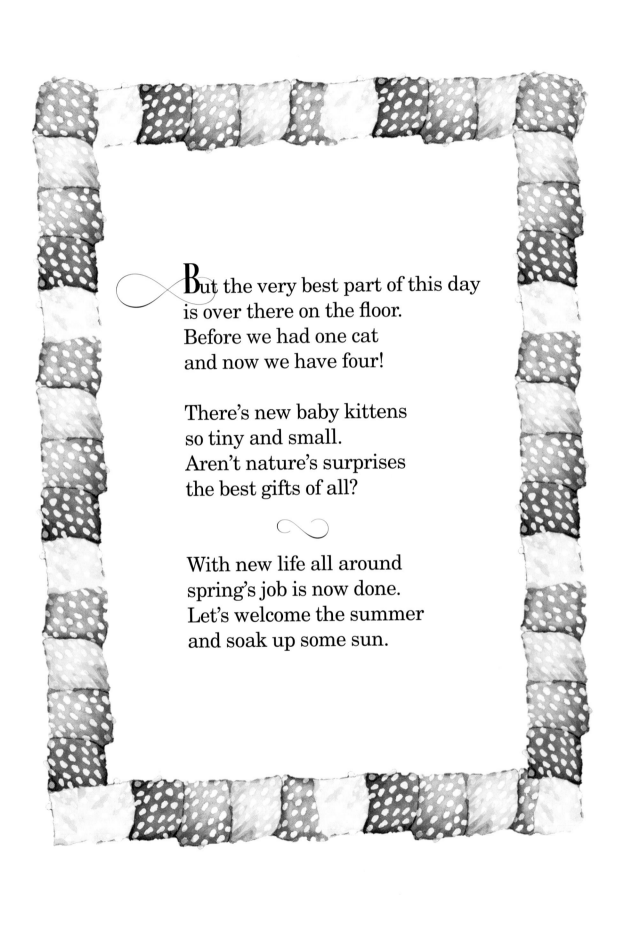

But the very best part of this day
is over there on the floor.
Before we had one cat
and now we have four!

There's new baby kittens
so tiny and small.
Aren't nature's surprises
the best gifts of all?

With new life all around
spring's job is now done.
Let's welcome the summer
and soak up some sun.

A hot summer's day,
let's try to stay cool
with fresh lemonade
and a jump in the pool!

When this summer day ends
with the sun still aglow,
there are memories to share
and treasures to show.

Snuggle up safe and warm,
as stars twinkle and play.
It's time to remember
the best part of the day.

Was it sand in our toes
or sand dunes to roam?

Was it fireflies flickering
all the way home?

Was it picking fresh veggies
right out of the ground?

Was it our picnic together
with good friends all around?

Whether winter or summer,
whether autumn or spring,
we all give our thanks
for the joy each day brings.

All small ones home now
to burrow, to hedge, to nest.
All babes in bed now
for cuddles, stories, and rest.

Snuggle up safe and sound,
for it's time to sleep tight.
We all say "I love you"
as we do every night.

It's the best part of the day!

Upon Reading This Book

We are ourselves our happiness

–LETITIA ELIZABETH LANDON (1825)

Welcome Dear Reader,

If you're a new acquaintance, I hope that by the end of our time together you'll think of me as a good friend. And if you're a cherished chum, welcome back. How wonderful to be in your company again!

Nearly twenty years ago I wrote a book for women called *Simple Abundance* that celebrates every woman's life in 366 daily essays on finding the sacred in the ordinary. *Simple Abundance: A Daybook of Comfort and Joy* became the classic bestseller story. Rejected thirty times over two years, it was finally published by Warner Books in November 1995 with little fanfare as "a woman's book." But women do love to talk to each other and within a few months it soon found its audience through word-of-mouth raves, including one from Oprah Winfrey who called it "life-changing." *Simple Abundance* claimed the top spot on the *New York Times* bestseller list in April 1996 and remained on the list for two consecutive years. It was also translated into twenty-eight different languages with international readers as far flung as Brazil and Japan. Still in print today, it reaches new readers every year and has sold more than eight million copies around the world.

The soul of *Simple Abundance* is the awareness that the active, daily practice of Gratitude can change our lives in miraculous ways. Women, possibly your own mother, bought the book to give to others for Christmas, birthdays, anniversaries, and graduations; in turn, women received it from family on Mother's Day, and their friends when their marriage ended, the job was eliminated, or the diagnosis was devastating. When a phone call sent a woman reeling, dashing her dreams and shattering the life she took for granted, the "pink book" turned up as often as casseroles.

Psychotherapists prescribed it to their patients; twelve-step program participants passed it on; abused women found it in a shelter's communal library; homeless women discovered it on their cots. Women read it while waiting to receive chemotherapy, then left it behind to the nurses who cared for them so tenderly. To celebrate, to commiserate, to comfort, to cheer, but above all to connect, women around the world—from Connecticut to Croatia to China—shared *Simple Abundance* with each other and blessed the life they found in between those pages—their own.

I have the same wonderful feeling about this sweet book called *The Best Part of the Day*. For many years readers have been asking me for a children's version of *Simple Abundance*. And while I wanted to write one, the search for the right format was rather like Goldilocks's search for the perfect chair. I couldn't find just the right fit.

That's because Gratitude is often thought of as an intellectual concept, when really Gratitude is a small seed planted in the heart that is nurtured and nourished through acknowledging all the good that surrounds us. Good that can be discovered through the reassuring comfort of family customs, rituals, and traditions and restoring a sense of rhythm in our daily round and through the changing seasons.

Each day all we have is all we need, although many days what we truly need is an awareness of how much we have. Gratitude makes this transformative miracle possible in tiny choices and small steps. The pace of Grace is best bestowed while holding a child's hand.

What I love best about *The Best Part of the Day* is that our happy task as we read to our children and grandchildren is to help them (as well as ourselves!) recall a few moments which brought smiles to their faces and made the day special. When we do this, we explore the grace of Gratitude, not as a "grown-up" philosophy, but as a creative and spiritual practice that anchors our lives in appreciation and wonder. The spontaneous glee of young children when exploring their bright new world—the splash of a pebble in a puddle, a ladybug on a leaf, the fog of breath on a winter's walk—seems very much what the thirteenth-century German mystic Meister Eckhart must have meant when he observed, "If the only prayer you ever say in your entire life is thank you, it will be enough."

It will be a personal joy if you and your family are as cheered by reading and playing *The Best Part of the Day* as I while working on this book. May you and yours have in the days and nights to come an abundance of cherished moments and memories inspired by seeking and celebrating the best part of every day.

Dearest love and blessings,

Sarah Ban Breathnach

What is the best part of your day?
Go online to www.RegneryKids.com to download
a beautiful Best Part of the Day journal activity.

Acknowledgments
With Thanks and Appreciation

It had been startling … to find
out that story books had been written by *people*,
that books were not natural wonders,
coming up of themselves like grass.

–EUDORA WELTY
ONE WRITER'S BEGINNINGS (1984)

I'm with Miss Welty: writing my first picture book has been a source of astonishing and continuous revelation. What do people have to do with story books?

Well, gratefully quite a lot. First of all, I'd like to thank my sister, Maureen O'Crean for helping me understand that writing for children is rather like felling a Redwood tree, then whittling it down with a paring knife to a toothpick. I have never written so many words that weren't included in the book before. Perhaps that's because the old adage, "A picture's worth a thousand words" is very true. So with deep gratitude, a bow to my brilliant and accomplished collaborator, the artist Wendy Edelson for never letting the brushstrokes show as she evoked such happy memories of both my daughter Kate and our English idyll at Newton's Chapel in England while we watched a natural wonder come beautifully into the world.

To the wonderful team I worked with at Regnery Kids, especially my editor, Diane Lindsey Reeves, who began our adventure with a charming offer that I simply couldn't refuse. Bless you, Diane, for writing one of the loveliest letters I've ever received. It reminded me that when we create from the heart miracles are possible. To Cheryl Barnes who worked so closely with Diane and introduced me to Wendy, thank you for such lovely match-making magic.

It's been an enchanting journey … and I hope we have many more sojourns together.

Also by Sarah Ban Breathnach

MRS. SHARP'S TRADITIONS:
Reviving Victorian Family Celebrations of Comfort and Joy

THE VICTORIAN NURSERY COMPANION:
A Posy for Parents, A Keepsake for Baby

SIMPLE ABUNDANCE:
A Daybook of Comfort and Joy

THE SIMPLE ABUNDANCE JOURNAL OF GRATITUDE

SOMETHING MORE:
Excavating Your Authentic Self

THE ILLUSTRATED DISCOVERY JOURNAL:
Creating a Visual Autobiography of Your Authentic Self

THE SIMPLE ABUNDANCE COMPANION
Following Your Authentic Path to Something More

A MAN'S JOURNEY TO SIMPLE ABUNDANCE

ROMANCING THE ORDINARY:
A Year of Simple Splendor

HOLD THAT THOUGHT:
A Year's Worth of Simple Abundance

MOVING ON:
Creating Your House of Belonging with Simple Abundance

PEACE AND PLENTY:
Finding Your Path to Financial Serenity

THE PEACE AND PLENTY JOURNAL OF WELL-SPENT MOMENTS